A Very Special Gift

VISTA
HIGHER LEARNING

Boston, Massachusetts

MATH

Martina is 15 years old. She lives in a nice house with her two younger sisters, her grandmother, and her grandfather. Her sister Rosa's seventh birthday is coming soon, and everyone is very excited.

Grandfather

Grandmother

Martina

Gabriela

Rosa

Martina wants to give Rosa a special present. Rosa has many superhero figures, but she has no place for them to live. Martina wants to buy a superhero house for Rosa, but the houses are too expensive. What can she do?

Martina tells her grandfather about her idea. "I can help," he says. "I have wood and tools. Let's build Rosa a superhero house together!"

house height = 36'
grandfather's height = 6'
36 ÷ 6 = 6
height ratio of 6:1

height ratio of 6:1
superhero's height = 4"
4" x 6 = 24" house height

roof

plan

ROSA'S HOUSE   39"

wall

24"

inch

floor

10 11 12 13 14

1" = 1 inch = 2.5 centimeters
1' = 1 foot = 12 inches

They make a **plan** for the house. "What should the **height** of the house be?" asks Martina.

"Well, our house is 36 feet tall," says Grandfather. "And I'm 6 feet tall. So, the **ratio** of our house to my height is six to one."

"OK. Rosa's favorite hero is about 4 inches tall," says Martina. "Four inches times 6 is 24 inches. Let's make the house 2 feet tall."

They decide to make the floor and roof longer and make them 39 inches long.

measure

thick

wide

$\frac{3}{4}$ = three **fourths**

Martina and her grandfather start to build the house. Grandfather has several long pieces of beautiful wood that are 12 inches **wide** and $\frac{3}{4}$ of an inch **thick**.

Grandfather **measures** 24 inches of wood. He marks the wood with a pencil and cuts the piece at the mark. It's their first wall!

"Now you try," says Grandfather. Martina measures 24 inches of wood and marks it with a pencil. She puts on goggles and gloves, and she carefully cuts the wood at the mark.

Grandfather looks at her work. "Very nice!" he says. Martina is very proud.

Martina cuts two more pieces of wood that are 39 inches long. One piece is for the roof and the other is for the floor.

Martina notices something.
She sees it and thinks about it.

Martina holds the wall pieces on the floor piece and glues them together. As she glues the roof piece on the top, Martina notices something. The house looks taller than what they had planned!

"Is this right, Grandfather?" she asks. "The house looks taller than 24 inches."

"Yes, it's fine," Grandfather answers.

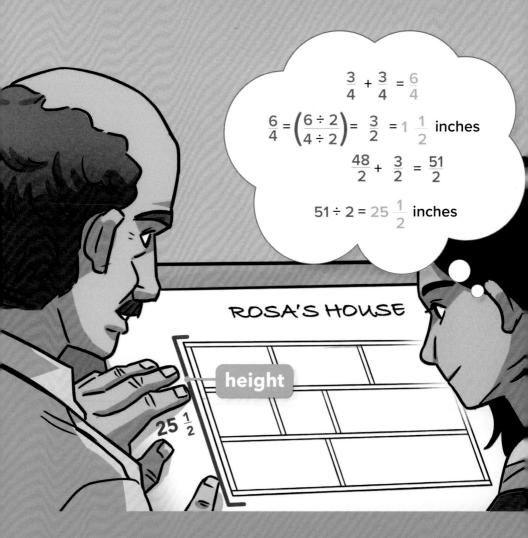

"The **thickness** of wood is $\frac{3}{4}$ of an inch," Grandfather explains. "The floor and roof each add $\frac{3}{4}$ of an inch. So how tall does that make the house?"

Martina thinks. "So, $\frac{3}{4}$ plus $\frac{3}{4}$. That's 6 fourths. We divide to **find the lowest terms**. Six fourths is the same as 3 **halves** or $1\frac{1}{2}$. The walls are 24 inches. That's the same as 48 halves, so we add 48 halves to 3 halves. That's 51 halves. We can divide to find the height. The house is $25\frac{1}{2}$ inches tall!" she says.

"Right!" says Grandfather.

There are three stories in the house. There are three floors.

Grandfather and Martina plan to have three stories in the house. Martina divides the height of the wall by three and figures out that each story will be 8 inches tall.

They must cut two more pieces of wood for the floors inside the house. "These pieces are the same as the first floor, right? So, they're 39 inches long?" asks Martina.

"No, they're not," answers Grandfather. Martina looks at her grandfather with surprise.

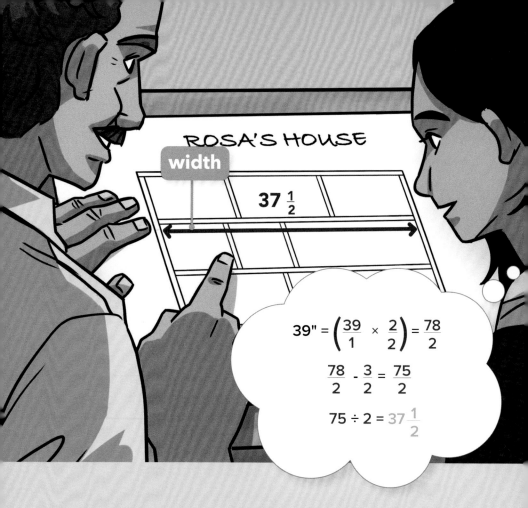

"Remember. The walls are $\frac{3}{4}$ of an inch thick," Grandfather explains. "They add $1\frac{1}{2}$ inches. We must subtract that from the **length** of the first floor."

"Oh, yeah," says Martina. "So, the first floor length is 39 inches. We want to take away 3 halves, so we need a **common denominator**. We multiply 39 over 1 by 2 over 2 and get 78 halves. Next, we take away 3 halves for the walls. We get 75 halves. We divide by 2 and get $37\frac{1}{2}$. So the second and third floors are $37\frac{1}{2}$ inches long. Is that right?"

"Right," answers Grandfather.

Martina cuts the floor pieces and glues them into the house. Next, Martina and her grandfather have to make walls for the rooms in the house. On the first floor there is a dining room and a kitchen. Martina cuts one wall to put between the two rooms. The wall is 8 inches tall and it fits perfectly as she puts it in place.

The pieces don't fit.
They're too big.

On the second floor there are three rooms: a
bathroom, a living room, and a science lab. Martina
cuts two more 8-inch pieces for walls. However,
when she puts them into the house, they don't fit.
She tries again, but they still don't go into place.
They're just too tall!

"Oh, no! I forgot!" says Martina. "The floors are $\frac{3}{4}$ of an inch thick. So, the second and third stories need to be shorter. I need to subtract $\frac{3}{4}$ of an inch from the height of 8 inches."

"That's right," says Grandfather with a smile. "The walls on the second and third floors are $7\frac{1}{4}$ inches tall, not 8. Let's try again."

Martina cuts the pieces again, and this time they fit.

There are two bedrooms on the top floor of the superhero house. They've even planned a room for the superhero airplane!

Grandfather and Martina get ready to cut two more pieces for the walls. They carefully measure $7\frac{1}{4}$ inches and cut the pieces. Martina places them between the second floor and the roof. The walls fit!

Martina and her grandfather finish the house. It's very beautiful!

A carpenter is a person who builds things with wood.

On the day of Rosa's birthday party, Martina gives Rosa her gift. "I love it!" says Rosa.

Martina looks at her grandfather and smiles. "The house is perfect," she says. "Thank you so much for your help!"

"You're very welcome, Martina," he says. "It was fun for me, too. You're really a great carpenter, and you made a wonderful house for your sister. It's much better than one from a store. It's a very special gift."

plan a drawing or guide for how to build or do something

height how tall something is

ratio a comparison of two amounts, we can multiply an amount by the ratio and keep the relationship the same

wide / width how far it is from one side of something to the other

one fourth, a fourth ($\frac{1}{4}$) one of four equal parts of a whole

thick / thickness how far it is from the bottom of something to the top

measure to check how big, small, light, or heavy something is

find the lowest terms to divide the top and bottom of a fraction by the same number

one half / a half ($\frac{1}{2}$) one of two equal parts of a whole

length how far it is from one end of something to the other

common denominator the bottom number in two fractions when that number is the same in both fractions